Instructions for using AR

LET AUGMENTED REALITY CHANGE HOW YOU READ A BOOK

With your smartphone, iPad or tablet you can use the **Neighbur Vue** app to invoke the augmented reality experience to literally read outside the book.

neighbur

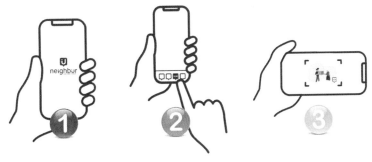

1. Notice the spelling: download the Neighbur Vue app from the Apple App Store or Google Play

2. Open and select the (vue) option

3. Point your lens at the full image with the and enjoy the augmented reality experience.

Go ahead and try it right now with the Hasmark Publishing International logo.

SHANTI'S SAFE PLACE

Yolanda Garner Hutcherson

ILLUSTRATED BY ARANAHAJ IQBAL

Hasmark
PUBLISHING
INTERNATIONAL

Published by
Hasmark Publishing
www.hasmarkpublishing.com

Copyright © 2021 Yolanda Hutcherson
First Edition

Disclaimer

This book is designed to provide information and motivation to our readers. It is sold with the understanding that the publisher is not engaged to render any type of psychological, legal, or any other kind of professional advice. The content of each article is the sole expression and opinion of its author, and not necessarily that of the publisher. No warranties or guarantees are expressed or implied by the publisher's choice to include any of the content in this volume. Neither the publisher nor the individual author(s) shall be liable for any physical, psychological, emotional, financial, or commercial damages, including, but not limited to, special, incidental, consequential or other damages. Our views and rights are the same: You are responsible for your own choices, actions, and results.

Permission should be addressed in writing to Yolanda at info@yolandahutcherson.com

Editor: Judith Scott
judith@hasmarkpublishing.com

Illustrations: Aranahaj Iqbal
aranahajillustration@gmail.com

Layout and Cover Design: Anne Karklins
anne@hasmarkpublishing.com

ISBN 13: 978-1-77482-041-4
ISBN 10: 1774820412

To my amazing husband, David;
our children, Ashanti and DJ; and my family.
To all the brave children, you are my heroes.

Shanti knew that another day had come from the chorus of little birds that always perched by her window. She tossed and turned, and she tried to block her ears from their song. Even though it was a bright and beautiful day, Shanti wasn't feeling too happy, but she knew she had no option but to go to school.

Slowly, she climbed out of bed and began to prepare for school. When she was done, Shanti strolled towards the kitchen.

Good morning, Mom," she said, and flashed a weak smile.

Mother returned her smile and quickly placed her breakfast on the table.

"How are you, Sweet Pea?"

Shanti ignored the question and began to quietly eat her cereal, while listening to her mother going on and on about the fun weekend trip they would have.

"I cannot wait for us to go to the cookout this weekend. It's going to be super fun! What do you think?" Mother asked.

Shanti pulled in a deep breath and forced another smile. "I think it would be very nice."

When she was done with her meal, she grabbed her bag and hugged her mother.

"Everyone is going to be at the cookout this weekend, so get ready to have fun!"

Shanti hugged her mother closely before releasing her and waving goodbye.

"Goodbye, Mommy!" Shanti smiled as she walked out of the house. "Goodbye, Shanti!" Mother waved back.

3

4

Shanti sighed as she stepped out of the house. The yellow sun was beginning to peek out of the clouds. It would be a very sunny day at school today.

But Shanti wasn't thinking about school. She was bothered about something else. Shanti's heart was beating fast as she thought about the cookout this weekend. "Would everyone really be there?" she whispered.

Soon, she caught a glimpse of the colorful flowers and butterflies that lined the sidewalks on the way to her elementary school. They were a welcome distraction. A smile played on her lips as she stared at the flowers. They were so beautiful. But the moment Shanti arrived at her class, she began to worry again.

She settled into her desk and began to tap her fingers on the surface. Usually, Shanti would say hello to her classmate, Emily, but Shanti wasn't in the right mood to talk today.

"Morning, Shanti. How are you?" Emily asked.

"I'm fine." Shanti replied, still tapping her fingers on the desk.

"What are you going to do this weekend?"

Shanti smiled. "Oh, my mother says there's a cookout this weekend and we are going."

Emily threw her hands into the air excitedly. "Wow! That sounds fun. I love cookouts," she said, hoping that Shanti would catch the fun in her tone.

However, Shanti wasn't thinking about all the fun they would have on that day. She was still thinking of all the people who she would see.

"Shanti?" Emily tapped her lightly on the arm.

"Um, sorry, I didn't hear you." Shanti sighed. She hadn't been listening to Emily.

"I was just excited about your cookout this weekend; all that food would be very delicious. Aren't you happy about it?" Emily wondered.

Shanti nodded. "Yes, I am. I can't wait to go." Shanti wasn't too thrilled by the idea, but she didn't want Emily to keep talking. She just wasn't in the mood for anything today.

Emily noticed this. "Are you all right?"

Shanti was about to answer when the class suddenly fell quiet.

Mr. McFarland had walked into the class with two women.

One of the women had beautiful curly hair. The other woman was tall and slender with a stern face. "Maybe they're new teachers," Shanti suggested.

"Good morning, class!" Mr. McFarland greeted them.

"Good morning!" the children chorused, while fixing their curious eyes on him.

Mr. McFarland knew that the kids were curious about the visitors. He could tell when they began to murmur among themselves.

So, he said, "Quiet now, and settle down. I know you are curious about my friends. Well, I will only introduce them if you listen to me."

The class fell quiet as they adjusted themselves in their seats and listened intently.

Mr. McFarland continued, "Remember I told you last week that we were going to have a special guest today. These people are here to talk to you about something that is very important. Please listen to them."

The kids kept their gazes on the women who were standing on either side of the computer board. "What you need to know to say no!" Shanti read aloud the words that were written on the board. "What does that even mean?" Emily wondered.

The woman with the curly hair was the first to step forward. She had a radiant smile on her face, and this caught the attention of the kids.

11

Hi, children! My name is Mrs. Walker, and I am a social worker." She paused and turned to the other woman.

"This is my friend, Detective Martinez. We want to talk to you today about something very important. The kids cheered and clapped; they were pleased to meet Mrs. Walker and Detective Martinez. Once the class was quiet, Mrs. Walker began.

"Who remembers when you were in first or second grade and you learned about stranger danger? We learned how it was important not to talk to strangers. Well, there can be times where people we know can also do harmful things to us, and that's what we've come to talk to you today.

"We know there are places on your body that people can touch and places that are private. Your private parts are places that no one should be touching. No adult should ask you to touch them on their private parts, either.

Class, direct your attention to this diagram," Mrs. Walker said. She pointed at the white board and the kids stared at the two figures on the board.

There were two figures, male and female.

"These are the areas that are private. Only your parents, caretakers, or doctors should touch you here, with your permission. If anyone touches you there, tell someone you trust, like your parent, a friend, or an adult."

Shanti held her breath as she listened. Sweat poured from the bridge of her nose to her upper lip.

"It doesn't matter if this person threatens to hurt you in any way. Do not be scared to speak out. We are here to help you," Mrs. Walker said. "We also help children in a special way if someone has touched their private parts. I am a social worker, so I help by talking to kids and their families to make sure that children are safe, get the right support, and guide them through the process if someone is doing things to their bodies that they don't like."

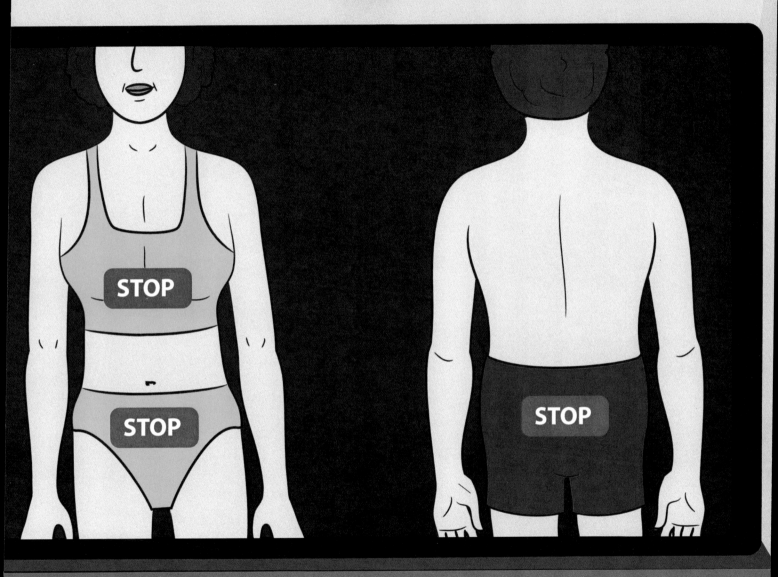

For the first time, Detective Martinez said something. "I am a Special Victims' Detective, a certain type of police officer who investigates cases with children when people do bad things like touch children's private parts. We both make sure children are safe. You can always report anyone who touches you in a bad way to us."

"I know what we talked about today is very important, but you are the guardians of your bodies. If you say no to someone, that means no!" Mrs. Walker smiled as she made her last statement.

The kids clapped and stared at both women.

The police officer smiled at the children and said, "If anyone has questions, feel free to ask. We love questions."

The kids didn't ask any questions, but they enjoyed the message that the women had shared with them. It was now time for the visitors to go.

Mr. McFarland turned to the visitors. "I really want to thank Mrs. Walker and Detective Martinez for coming this morning and sharing about how they protect children. Most importantly, giving us information about our bodies and how to keep them safe."

As the adults walked out of the class, Shanti pulled in a deep breath and rose to her feet. She had a private question about something that had been bothering her.

20

Hi, I am Shanti. I have something to ask you, if you have time?" she asked in a fearful and shaky voice. Mrs. Walker and Detective Martinez were standing alone with her in the hallway.

"Come with us so we can talk," Mrs. Walker said as she touched Shanti's shoulder gently. Mr. McFarland escorted them down the hall.

The women decided to have a private discussion with Shanti in the school clinic. The nurse's office was empty, so they all walked in and sat down.

Mrs. Walker broke the silence. "Tell us what's on your mind."

Shanti nodded and began, "Well, my cousin Corey touched me on places he is not supposed to. My parents don't know about this, and I think they will be upset."

"Okay, tell you what? Let's call your parents and see if we can help," Detective Martinez suggested. "This way we can introduce ourselves."

Shanti thought that this was a good suggestion.

Shanti's mother had been busy at home when her phone rang. She grabbed it and placed it against her ear. "Hello, is this Mrs. Glass…Shanti's mother?"

Shanti's mother nodded. "Yes, this is her."

"My name is Mrs. Walker and I am a social worker with Child Services. I spoke with Shanti today in school and wanted to see if you could bring her to my office tomorrow so that we could talk.

At first Shanti's mother was afraid.

"Did something happen to my daughter? Hello?"

"Not at all, ma'am, but we really need to talk to you and Shanti."

"Okay," Mrs. Glass said as she wrote down Mrs. Walker's address.

The next day, Mrs. Glass was very nervous about what Mrs. Walker had said, but she was careful not to say that she was. Together, she and Shanti left for Mrs. Walker's office.

28

CHILD SAFE CENTER

Hello, Mrs. Glass, I am Mrs. Walker, and this is Detective Martinez. We were invited to the school yesterday to talk to your daughter's class about body safety. Shanti came to us and wanted to ask a few questions, but what she told us was concerning. So, thanks for bringing her in so that I could talk to her.

"Shanti, come with me so that we can continue our conversation we had yesterday," Mrs. Walker said. "I want you to be comfortable and know that we are here for you."

Shanti started to fiddle with her fingers and started to talk.

"A few weeks ago, my cousin was at my house babysitting me while my parents went to the movies. I wanted to go swimming in the pool, so we went to the basement to get a float. He asked me to play a game and if I played it, then he would buy me ice cream later. I said 'sure' but he said I would have to take off my swimsuit, and I said 'no.' That's when he grabbed my arm and touched me on the area you said we are not supposed to be touched. When he grabbed me, he broke the bracelet that my mom gave me for my birthday. That is when I picked up the broken beads off the floor. He told me not to say anything because no one would believe me."

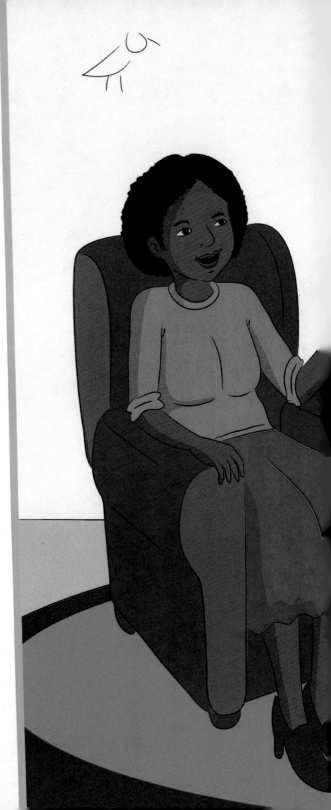

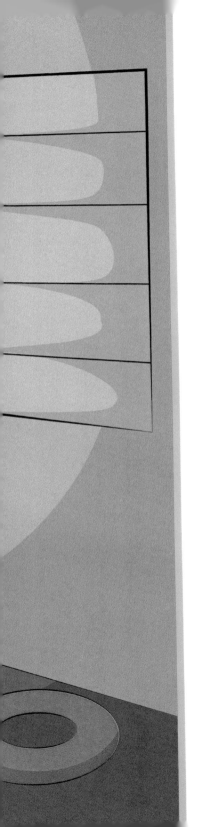

Once she was done telling her story, she felt better, but she was thinking about her broken bracelet.

"I am sorry that you had to go through this. You are such a brave girl, Shanti. Are you ready to share this with your mother?" Mrs. Walker asked.

Once they were outside the room, Shanti walked towards her mother and decided to share the story.

"Mommy, I have to tell you something. You know when you and daddy went to the movies and Corey babysat me? Well, he touched me on my private areas. I didn't say anything because he said that you wouldn't believe me."

Tears rushed down her mother's cheeks as she heard the story, but she quickly wiped them off.

"He also broke the bracelet that you gave to me. I picked up the pieces, and I put them in my jewelry box. I tried to put it back together on my own, but I couldn't."

When Shanti finished telling her story, her mother rose to her feet and hugged her tightly. "I am so sorry for not being there to protect you. I promise that no one will ever hurt you again!" Shanti smiled and hugged her mother tightly. She felt loved and cared about.

They both walked out of the office feeling happy and relaxed.

Once they reached home, Shanti pulled out her broken bracelet and its pieces. She and her mother began to work on the bracelet.

Mother couldn't stop smiling at her baby girl.

"You know you did the right thing by saying something today. I am proud of you. Now let's get this bracelet fixed so you can wear it again."

Shanti couldn't wait to wear her bracelet. She was no longer worried about anything, because she had shared her story. It is good to talk to someone when we have been touched in the wrong places. Always remember to say No! Do not be afraid to speak out!

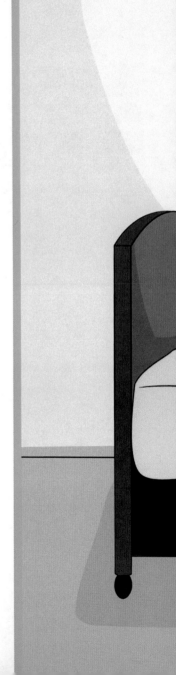

Acknowledgements

I wrote this book a few years ago, and it sat in my computer until I was ready to share it. The work that I do with families and children inspired me to tell this story.

To all my coworkers at Nassau County Department of Social Services, Nassau County Police Department (Special Victims Department), my local Child Advocacy Center, and all MDT partners. Your work with children and families is amazing.

To my illustrator, Aranahaj Illustrations, for your help, patience, and bringing my vision to life.

Thank you to my husband, David, who supports all my dreams and encourages me.

Thank you to my children, Ashanti and DJ, who are my biggest cheerleaders.

To my parents, for giving me a solid family foundation and encouraging me to be what I want.

To my bonus mom, Ruby, for your prayers and support.

Thank you to my circle of friends and family who encourage me to do what I do, because I love it.

About the Author

"If you don't heal the wounds of your childhood, you bleed into the future..."
– Oprah Winfrey

Yolanda Garner Hutcherson has over 10 years of experience in the social work field and is an influencer, author, podcaster, and speaker. Yolanda was born and raised in Hempstead, New York. She lives in New York with her husband and their two children.

Yolanda comes from a long legacy of entrepreneurs, serving as the President of a 30-year family-owned business. Yolanda is a graduate of an HBCU (Historically Black Colleges & Universities), North Carolina Central University, and holds a Masters in Social Work from Adelphi University.

Yolanda's career has centered around child welfare, inspired by her own experience of sexual abuse as a child by a family member. She has worked tirelessly for years in the field, and at present she investigates sex abuse cases involving children.

As an aside to this, Yolanda is also a first-time author and is excited about this new chapter in her life, where she aims to bring the important matter of child sexual abuse to the forefront of as many people's minds as possible.

Her hopes for the future are to continue to work and advocate for vulnerable children, to write more books on this vital subject, and to travel the world sharing her knowledge of it with others.

You can contact Yolanda Garner Hutcherson at info@yolandahutcherson.com
or through her website at http://yolandahutcherson.com/
Instagram: @garneringgreatness   Facebook: Garnering Greatness

With every donation, a voice will be given to
the creativity that lies within the hearts of
our children living with diverse challenges.

By making this difference, children that may
not have been given the opportunity to have their
Heart Heard will have the freedom to create
beautiful works of art and musical creations.

Donate by visiting

HeartstobeHeard.com

We thank you.

Made in the USA
Las Vegas, NV
18 May 2021